Dear Parents:

Congratulations! Your child is taking the first steps on an exciting journey. The destination? Independent reading!

STEP INTO READING® will help your child get there. The program offers five steps to reading success. Each step includes fun stories and colorful art or photographs. In addition to original fiction and books with favorite characters, there are Step into Reading Non-Fiction Readers, Phonics Readers and Boxed Sets, Sticker Readers, and Comic Readers—a complete literacy program with something to interest every child.

Learning to Read, Step by Step!

Ready to Read   Preschool–Kindergarten
• big type and easy words • rhyme and rhythm • picture clues
For children who know the alphabet and are eager to begin reading.

Reading with Help   Preschool–Grade 1
• basic vocabulary • short sentences • simple stories
For children who recognize familiar words and sound out new words with help.

Reading on Your Own   Grades 1–3
• engaging characters • easy-to-follow plots • popular topics
For children who are ready to read on their own.

Reading Paragraphs   Grades 2–3
• challenging vocabulary • short paragraphs • exciting stories
For newly independent readers who read simple sentences with confidence.

Ready for Chapters   Grades 2–4
• chapters • longer paragraphs • full-color art
For children who want to take the plunge into chapter books but still like colorful pictures.

STEP INTO READING® is designed to give every child a successful reading experience. The grade levels are only guides; children will progress through the steps at their own speed, developing confidence in their reading.

Remember, a lifetime love of reading starts with a single step!

Copyright © 2016 Disney Enterprises, Inc. All rights reserved. Published in the United States by Random House Children's Books, a division of Penguin Random House LLC, 1745 Broadway, New York, NY 10019, and in Canada by Random House of Canada, a division of Penguin Random House Ltd., Toronto, in conjunction with Disney Enterprises, Inc.

Step into Reading, Random House, and the Random House colophon are registered trademarks of Penguin Random House LLC.

Visit us on the Web!
StepIntoReading.com
randomhousekids.com

Educators and librarians, for a variety of teaching tools, visit us at RHTeachersLibrarians.com

ISBN 978-0-7364-3450-8 (trade) — ISBN 978-0-7364-8214-1 (lib. bdg.)
ISBN 978-0-7364-3451-5 (ebook)

Printed in the United States of America   10 9 8 7 6 5 4 3 2 1

Disney

Whisker Haven
TALES
with the
palace pets

The Knight Night Guard

By Amy Sky Koster

Illustrated by the Disney Storybook Art Team

Random House 🏠 New York

It is a sunny day
in Whisker Haven.
Pumpkin is dressing up.

Roar!

Sultan leaps

into the room.

Sultan is dressed up
as the Knight Night Guard.
The Knight Night Guard
is the bravest pet
in Whisker Haven.

Treasure is dressed
up as the Knight Night
Guard, too!

Sultan says

he is the bravest pet.

Treasure says

she is the bravest pet.

They will have a contest!

Pumpkin will judge.

First, the pets
must be brave
in the dark!

Boom!
Crack!

Pumpkin is scared.
Sultan and Treasure
are not.

Spiders are next!

Pumpkin is scared.

Sultan and Treasure
are not.

The pets hear a growl!
Sultan and Treasure
are scared.
Pumpkin is not.
She knows that sound!

Pumpkin says
there is a beast.
The pet who is
not afraid will be the
Knight Night Guard.

Sultan and Treasure
follow the sound.

They see a monster!

They run!

The monster is Dreamy!
She is snoring.

Sultan and Treasure
go back.

Pumpkin was not scared.
She is the new
Knight Night Guard!

Pumpkin gets a helmet
and body armor.

Hooray for the new Whisker Haven Knight Night Guard!